A DE RUSSE CHRISTMAS MIRACLE

A MEDIEVAL ROMANCE

BY KATHRYN LE VEQUE

KATHRYN LE VEQUE NOVELS

Kathlyn Trent/Marcus Burton Series:

Valley of the Shadow

The Eden Factor

Canyon of the Sphinx

The American Heroes Anthology Series:

The Lucius Robe

Fires of Autumn

Evenshade

Sea of Dreams

Purgatory

Other non-connected Contemporary Romance:

Lady of Heaven

Darkling, I Listen

In the Dreaming Hour

River's End

The Fountain

Sons of Poseidon:

The Immortal Sea

Pirates of Britannia Series (with Eliza Knight):

Savage of the Sea by Eliza Knight

Leader of Titans by Kathryn Le Veque

The Sea Devil by Eliza Knight

Sea Wolfe by Kathryn Le Veque

Note: All Kathryn's novels are designed to be read as stand-alones, although many have cross-over characters or cross-over family groups. Novels that are grouped together have related characters or family groups. You will notice that some series have the same books; that is because they are cross-overs. A hero in one book may be the secondary character in another.

There is NO reading order except by chronology, but even in that case, you can still read the books as stand-alones. No novel is connected to another by a cliff hanger, and every book has an HEA.

Series are clearly marked. All series contain the same characters or family groups except the American Heroes Series, which is an anthology with unrelated characters.

For more information, find it in **A Reader's Guide to the Medieval World of Le Veque**.

TABLE OF CONTENTS

Author's Note

I have such fun writing these little holiday stories! It's so much fun to bring together some of my favorite families, seeing them all in one place, interacting. This particular tale is meant as an extended epilogue to DARK MOON and DARK STEEL, set in the year following Dane and Grier's story in DARK STEEL. You don't have to read those two stories to know what's going on, but it would help orient the reader.

Much like "A Joyous de Wolfe Christmas", this story is meant as a focus on one particularly thing – in this case, the illness of Gaston de Russe (THE DARK ONE: DARK KNIGHT). Gaston's illness was introduced in DARK MOON, and elaborated on in DARK STEEL, so now we have it as the focus of the story. As much as I hate to see my heroes and heroines get old, the truth is that they do, and especially if I'm writing about the children and grandchildren of original heroes and heroines. That's a fact of life. But I promise I will never actually write their death scenes – that's something I can't bring myself to do.

Something fun to note – there is another Father de Tormo in this tale, the younger brother of Father de Tormo from THE DARK ONE: DARK KNIGHT. Interestingly enough, I never gave the original Father a first name in the book – and

I had to go back into my VERY old notes to find it. So, the Father de Tormo in this tale is a brother, and it was fun to bring the de Tormo name back into a de Russe story.

I don't normally write religious-themed stories, and I don't consider this one, but I do consider it a story of faith. Faith in love, faith in family, and faith in a higher power. It brings about the question – *are* there miracles? Or can everything be scientifically explained away? That's something Dane and Trenton and Remington have to figure out for themselves.

You be the judge.

Love,

Kathryn

PART ONE:
A BRIGHT AND SHINING STAR

Wiltshire

December, Year of Our Lord 1520

I T WAS BRIGHT enough, with a winter-white landscape spread out before them like the frosting on a sweetcake. White as far as the eye could see, but in the sky above, the blue was the most vibrant of blues. It was the holiday season, and Dane de Russe, Duke of Shrewsbury, and his lady wife, Grier, were traveling south to Deverill Castle to celebrate the season with Dane's family.

The seat of the Duke of Warminster, Gaston de Russe, was a vast complex of buildings, men, and animals, and even now, Dane knew it was stuffed to the gills with his brothers, sisters, and their families. All told, there were more than two dozen of them, as he'd been trying to tell his wife on the ride south.

Grier was bundled up against the cold, wrapped heavily

in furs and wool, and her beautiful face was pinched red from the cold. But she was radiant, happier than Dane had ever seen her. She had been talking up a storm for most of the trip, too, which had taken seven days so far because Dane had wanted to take it slow. He didn't want his pregnant wife jostled around, but Grier was made of iron. Nothing bothered her, and she didn't care if the road was muddy or icy and they were forced to take a precious hour to go around it.

She was joy personified.

"Tell me again," she said, her head sticking out of the heavy carriage she was riding in as Dane rode alongside on his big-boned rouncey. "Your eldest sisters and their families?"

Dane signed heavily, an exaggerated gesture. "Again?"

"Again."

"But I told you not two hours ago," he pointed out. "I swear, you do not remember anything I tell you these days."

She grinned and sat back in the cab, her hand on her belly. At six months along, she was healthy and rosy. "This child sucks all of the thoughts straight out of my head," she said. "I cannot remember anything that anyone has told me, so do not feel as if you are special in that regard."

He cocked a droll eyebrow at her. "One more time," he said. "If you do not remember this time, then I shall not tell you again and you can fumble your way through your first conversation with my family and look like an idiot. Everyone will say what a beautiful dolt I have married."

She giggled. "I will remember. Go on."

He growled again, which just made her giggle more. "My brother, Trenton, is married to Lysabel Wellesbourne," he said. "You already know that."

"I do."

"You know that Lysabel has two daughters from her first marriage, and she gave birth to my brother's firstborn son during the summer."

"Aye, I remember. His name is Rafael."

"Correct," Dane said. "My sisters, Adeliza and Arica, are twins, and Adeliza is married to Gaspard de Ryes, a knight in the service of King Henry. I cannot imagine Gaspard will be at Deverill, as Henry keeps him quite busy, but Adeliza will be present, no doubt. They have six girls – do you remember their names?"

Grier thought very hard. "Madalene, Marguerite, Remy, Cassandra, Nynette, and Rosemarie?"

He grunted. "You can remember the children's names, but nothing else?"

"That is because I have my own child to name. A name means something."

Dane fought off a grin as he looked away. "His name will be Dane," he said. "There is nothing to discuss."

She simply lifted her eyebrows. "I like the name Brandt," she said. "You said that all of the men in the de Russe family have the same name – Brandt, Hugh, Braxton, Gaston,

Trenton, and so forth. And I like Brandt."

"We shall see who wins this battle."

"Aye, we shall see."

He turned to look at her, thinking to give her a threatening glare, but she stuck her tongue out at him and he started laughing. "Saucy wench," he said, sounding resigned. "Shall I continue? Arica is married to Sir Damien Delamere, a knight with the House of de Lohr. I am not certain he will be here, either, but it is possible. They have three boys and two girls. Don't tell me you remember *their* names."

Grier nodded firmly. "Bryant, Etienne, Henry, Elise, and Nicola."

"Very good. Cort has no children, nor do Boden, Gage, and Gilliana, but my brother, Matthieu, does. He has four sons."

She hung her head from the carriage again. "I know," she said. "Braxton, Hugh, Gaston, and Lucien."

"But remember that his wife died two years ago, so unless he brings it up, do not speak of it."

"I will not, I promise."

Dane's eyes glimmered at her. "You know everyone who will be there," he said. "Although I have a feeling Uncle Matthew and Aunt Alix will be there as well, and if they bring their brood, then it will be a crowd like you have never seen before."

Grier watched as the warmth faded from his features, replaced by the same concern and grief that seemed to fill his expression whenever the subject of his father came up. The man was sick, and had been for some time, with a cancer in his throat. At least, that's what the physics said. But Gaston was a strong man; stronger than most. Cancer or no cancer, he refused to let it slow him down. But over the past year, no matter how hard he'd tried, it was evident that he was slowing down a great deal.

But his sons, like Dane, simply couldn't take it.

The strongest man they knew was fading.

"Do you think it will be too much for your father?" she asked quietly. "Surely all of those people will overtax him."

Dane shook his head before she even finished. "It is the best medicine in the world for him, being surrounded by those he loves," he said. He looked to his wife as she sat in the cab, her hand on her belly. "And we've not told him about this child. It will be the best Christmas gift that we can give him."

Grier smiled timidly. "I hope so," she said. "I worry that it will be too exhausting for so many people to be at Deverill."

Dane sighed faintly, his gaze moving over the winter-white landscape. "No one wants to miss this Christmas," he said. "It may be the very last one my father ever has. I, for one, wouldn't miss it for anything."

Grier could hear the pain in his voice. "And we shall not," she said confidently. "I am very much looking forward to telling your father of our Christmas present to him. But most importantly, he must be here when it is opened. I should like for him to be one of the first ones to hold your son."

Dane smiled bravely at her, but the tears were there at the thought of his father holding his grandson for the first time. It was like an arrow to his heart, so bittersweet he could barely stand it.

"As would I," he said hoarsely.

Grier reached a hand out to him from the cab window and he took it, bending over to kiss it sweetly before letting it go. The feeling, for Dane's father, was mutual between them.

After that, the conversation fell silent for the most part as they neared the town of Warminster. Deverill Castle was to the south of the town, but not very far away. The day was waning and dusk was approaching, but Dane was certain they would make it by nightfall, if not just before.

Thankfully, the sky had remained clear in spite of the snow and cold temperatures, but the travel hadn't been uncomfortable in the least, which was a good thing. It could have been a blizzard and Dane still would have fought to make it home this time.

One last Christmas with his father.

The sky was darkening as they entered the northern out-skirts of Warminster. The land was relatively flat here but for a few hills now and again, rising out of the greenery like silent sentinels. To the east, a few clouds were starting to show and the further they traveled, the more the clouds seemed to gather. They hadn't quite moved in their direction yet, but Dane suspected they soon would. Still, they would be at Deverill Castle and the weather gods could bring all the snow they wanted to at that point. A white Christmas was a beautiful thing to see.

Entering the town proper, the smell of smoke from cooking fires wafted in the air. There were a few homes on the outskirts, all of them preparing for the coming night. As the party continued on, a church rose up on the bend of the road, a stone structure with moss growing on the walls. A churchyard spread out around it, with the tips of gravestones sticking up through the snow.

"Dane?"

Grier was calling him from the cab and Dane reined his horse around, trotting back to the carriage where she had her head out of the window again. She was smiling.

"Warminster, I presume?" she asked.

He nodded. "Indeed," he said. "Deverill Castle is less than an hour away now. We are very close."

Grier nodded as she looked around, her rosy face the only thing visible beneath the fur hood she wore. "It does not look like a very big town," she said. "Not as big as Shrewsbury."

Dane was looking around, too. "We are on the very northern edge," he told her. "It becomes much bigger the further south we go."

From the window on the opposite side of the cab, Grier

had caught sight of the church and she moved across the bench, sticking her head out so she could view the church in full.

"What church is that?" she asked.

Dane came to the other side of the carriage. "That is St. Denys," he said. "In fact, my younger siblings were all baptized there. Deverill Castle does not have its own chapel, so this is where the family conducts its religious business. My mother and father, though not particularly religious people, are nonetheless great patrons of the church. Since my father is the duke, it is expected."

Grier's gaze was still on the mossy-stoned building. "It looks as if it is very old."

"It is." Dane took a second look at the building. "In fact, I should stop in to see the priest. He is a good friend of my father's, a brother of a priest who was a dear friend to both my mother and father many years ago. His name is de Tormo."

Grier looked at him. "De Tormo," she repeated. "Where have I heard that name?"

He grinned. "From me," he said. "That was the priest who helped my mother and father get church approval to wed. You remember the story; my mother was married to the man whose blood I carry, Guy Stoneley, and my father was in love with her. It was Father de Tormo, who had been a papal envoy at the time, who helped my mother and father finally marry. Because my parents owed the man so much, they gave his younger brother this parish with their rich patronage. He has been here for at least twenty years."

Grier smiled at him. "Then go in and see him," she said. "I shall wait for you here."

"You do not wish to go in with me?"

She shook her head. "I have so many furs on me that I could not possibly get out of this cab," she said, watching him laugh. "I am warm and content. Go in and see the priest. I shall wait for you here."

He nodded as he dismounted his steed. "I shall only be a minute."

Grier watched her handsome husband, deeply in love with the man from the top of his cropped blond head to the bottom of his booted feet.

As the heiress to the duchy of Shrewsbury, she'd been an oblate pledged to St. Idloe's Abbey last year when she had received word that her deceased father had pledged her to a powerful young warlord. It hadn't been the life Grier had wanted, nor had it been the life Dane had wanted, but the two of them married out of obligation. After a rather rocky start, they were happier now than they'd ever been, and Grier knew how important this trip home was for Dane. She also knew that there were, perhaps, some things he'd rather do alone, like visit a church where his father was a patron and, perhaps, say a prayer for the man's health.

If he needed her, he would let her know.

So, she sat back in the cab, blowing a kiss to her husband

as he winked at her before making his way through the snow and into the church. Dane had brought a big escort with him from Shrewsbury, so he didn't worry for his wife's safety as he trudged through the snow, through a path that had been cleared by the acolytes. Tomorrow was Christmas, after all, and tonight, the faithful would be coming for Christmas Eve mass.

But Dane had a very special reason for visiting the church on this eve.

There was something he had to do.

Pushing open the doors of the church, Dane was met with the strong smell of rushes, as pine boughs lined the walls and floor on the perimeter of the church. Passing through the nave, he entered the chapel proper, with its dirt floors and tall windows inlaid with precious colored glass.

He remembered the church from his youth, and from the years he'd spent as his father's captain of the army, and the place held fond memories for him. He was on the hunt for Father de Tormo, seeing acolytes further forward in the quire, but not seeing the priest. He was heading for the acolytes, preparing for Christmas Eve mass, when a round figure in heavy robes came in through the door that led outside to the small cloister. Dane immediately recognized the man he sought.

He was in for a rather enthusiastic greeting.

FERDINAND DE TORMO was a man on a mission. He'd seen the Shrewsbury escort outside the church and was hoping that he might catch sight of the new duke. He'd heard all about the man from his father and mother, and he was quite excited that the stalwart young knight who had so ably commanded Warminster's armies was now a duke in his own right. He came flying in through the door, as fast as his legs would carry him, rushing right at Dane.

"My lord!" he said, gasping for air because he was quite heavy. "You have returned! God be praised!"

Dane had to grin at the round priest as the man shuffled in his direction. He caught a distinct whiff of foul body odor as the man drew near, and even tried to step away, but the priest wouldn't hear of it. It wasn't exactly protocol to hug a duke, but Father de Tormo did just that. He hugged Dane so hard that the man grunted.

"It is good to see you, too," Dane said, discreetly pulling himself away from the slightly moldy smelling priest. "It has been at least two years, hasn't it?"

De Tormo nodded eagerly. "Two years and a few months," he said. "How goes it in Shrewsbury? It is all your mother can speak of. She tells me that you have married."

Dane nodded. "I have," he said. "In fact, my wife is with me, but she is in the carriage outside. It was too cold for her to come traipsing in here through the snow. We are on our way to Deverill to see my family for Christmas."

De Tormo beamed, a gap-toothed smile that was infectious. He was a genuinely kind man and his flock adored him.

"Your mother and father will be so very happy," he said. "Do they know you are coming?"

"They do."

"Excellent. I have mass tonight and tomorrow, but I thought to go out later in the morning to visit your father." His smile faded. "Your father does not come to church any longer. I go to the castle a few times a month to hear his confession and speak with him. He is as sharp as ever."

At the mention of his father's fading health, Dane could feel his good mood fading. "I have not seen my father in almost a year," he said. "I stopped here because I thought you could give me a truthful answer on his health. My mother will make it sound not too terribly bad, my brothers will make it sound horrible, so I thought you could tell me the truth. How *is* my father?"

De Tormo drew in a long, slow breath. "I am not a physic, Dane."

"I know. But you have been around him."

De Tormo averted his gaze. "From what I have seen, he is not well," he said with regret. "Your father was always the biggest man I've ever seen, tall and proud and strong. Fearsome in battle, I am told."

Dane nodded reverently. "He was," he murmured. "I had the privilege of fighting with him a few times. There is no one fiercer. Men flee from my father as if the Devil himself has just appeared on the battlefield."

De Tormo had known Dane for many years. He knew how much Gaston de Russe's sons loved their father, and how much respect there was. To see the old knight fading away was truly a tragedy, in many aspects, but the tragedy was never more evident than it was when he looked in Dane's eyes.

That was where the true sorrow was.

"Then he has a fine legacy to remember and great sons to carry on his name," he said, trying to be of some comfort. "I have seen Trenton. Your older brother was here only yesterday along with his wife and children. I had much the same conversation with him. And Cort and Matthieu, Boden and Gage – I have seen all of your younger brothers here as of late, at one time or another. They are all worried about your father, Dane, and I will tell you what I have told them – go home and be with him. No man truly knows how much time he has left in this world but, with your father, I suspect his time will come to an end soon. Make sure you are there when it does. Tell him how much you love him and tell him you will carry on the de Russe name with pride."

By that time, Dane was fighting off tears. That's not what he had wanted to hear, but it was not unexpected. When he looked at de Tormo, it was with great mourning in his expression.

"I stopped here on my way to Deverill because I want to light a candle for my father and ask you to pray for him," he said. "I... I have not prayed in years, Father. My wife is a former oblate, and she prays regularly, but I do not. I have not since I was young and I suppose it is because I saw the evil of this world at a very young age. Often, I saw my mother pray for the evil to stop, but it never did. I learned long ago that God does not listen to my mother or to me."

De Tormo knew of Dane's past, mostly because his own past was rather intertwined with it to a certain extent. His brother had been a papal envoy who had ended up befriending Gaston at a time when he'd met his wife, Remington. Dane had been very young, and Remington had been married to Dane's father, a man more vile than words could express. When he wasn't beating his wife and her sisters, who were his wards, Guy Stoneley was raping them and otherwise degrading them.

Indeed, vile didn't quite cover the deeds of the man who had fathered Dane. That was where de Tormo's brother had come in, and although he'd died before he finally saw Gaston and Remington wed, his work on behalf of the couple, to obtain a divorce for Remington, was something Gaston had never forgotten. That was why Ferdinand had received his post at St. Denys – it had been Gaston's way of thanking his brother for everything he'd done, and everything the couple had put him through.

But the fact remained that the de Russe family and the de Tormo brothers were inexorably intertwined, for better or for worse, and that was how Ferdinand knew so much about the family.

It was his duty to guide them in matters of religion, whether or not they were religious.

"My lord, I understand your relationship with God has not been a strong one," he said after a moment. "I understand that you believe God does not listen. I assure you that He does, and He does, indeed, answer prayers, even if the answer is sometimes 'no'. I have told your mother that, many times, for she still does not have strength of faith, and that lack of faith has rubbed off on you. How can I tell you that your prayers to God about your father will be heard far more strongly than mine?"

Dane's brow furrowed. "How is that so? You are closer to God than I am."

De Tormo smiled faintly. "But you love Gaston, and love is very similar to faith. You believe in its strength; it has never failed you. Jesus said that if you have faith as small as a mustard seed, you can move mountains. And I believe love is just as strong as faith – it can move mountains. It can bring about change. It can make miracles happen."

Dane pondered that for a moment but, ultimately, he wasn't comfortable with prayer. "Mayhap," he said quietly. "But I still do not believe God listens to me. Would you please say a prayer for my father tonight? On this most holy of nights, mayhap God will listen particularly close."

De Tormo put his hands upon Dane's armored forearm. "Listen to me, Dane," he said with quiet assurance. "Say a prayer for your father yourself. Do not trust something so important to others. Your love for the man will cause God to hear you loudly. Please try."

Dane was starting to waver. Doubtfully, he looked at the front of the church, where the altar was, and the he looked to the prayer nave against one wall, the one that held dozens of candles, some of them lit. He knew they were prayer candles and each one represented a specific prayer from someone in great need. Well, *he* was in great need, too.

He needed his father to be healed.

With the greatest reluctance, he nodded his head at de Tormo and headed over to the banks of candles against the wall. There was no one around, and it was only his footsteps falling upon the fresh boughs. He stood there a moment, unsure what to do, before finally picking up an already-burning candle and lighting a dark candle in the front row. Once the flame ignited, he put the other candle back into its holder and took a deep breath.

"I do not know where to begin," he muttered. "I have not spoken to you in many years. I grew up believing you did not care for me or my mother. Will you listen to me now? I do not know why you should. I have never blasphemed you, but I have never sung your praises, either."

He fell silent, looking around the church, noticing that de Tormo had disappeared. Knowing he was alone made it easier to say what needed to be said.

"God, I hope you hear me," he said. "I have never asked

for anything, but this time, I am. I am asking you to heal my father. He is greatly loved, God. He has children and grandchildren who need him and love him. My father was not always a man of love and peace. I am sure you know that; he was a man of war. But my father was never deliberately evil. He was a man with principles. I know he has a reputation as the Dark One, and that has followed him around most of his life, but he is not dark. He is not wicked. I know that because he saved my mother and me from a man who was truly wicked. He risked everything for us and, to me, that is the mark of a fine and decent man, no matter what others think of him. God... there are many men in the world, but only one Gaston de Russe. I know I am a grown man, but I cannot stomach the thought of losing the only man who has ever loved me unconditionally. I would gladly trade my life for his. Please... heal him."

By the time he was finished, he was choked up. The tears were on the surface and he swiftly wiped them away. Feeling somewhat foolish that he'd been speaking in the dark, to a God he didn't have a relationship with, he stepped back from the bank of candles, looking around to see if there was anyone in the chapel who might have heard him. But it was still dark and empty.

Dane knew that Grier was waiting patiently for him outside and he didn't want to leave her in the cold too much longer, but something was keeping him in the church. He just couldn't seem to leave. He stared at his prayer candle as it flickered before impulsively dropping to his knees and making the sign of the cross over his chest. He hadn't done that since he'd been a small boy. On his knees in front of the glowing bank of candles and their warm light, he folded his hands and closed his eyes.

"Please," he whispered fervently. "God, I kneel before you as a sign of respect. I cannot promise that my faith will ever be strong, but I do have faith in my love for my father. There is no stronger bond than that between a man and his son, and since you had a son, you understand what I mean. I ask you to heal my father and to make him whole or, at the very least, let him live to see my son when he is born. My father means so much to so many. We need him, God. Please… please give us that gift. On this night of nights, give me my father's life."

With that, he suddenly lurched to his feet and blindly turned for the church entry. There were tears clouding his vision and he blinked them away. He was embarrassed and, perhaps, even a little bewildered. He'd prayed, and that was so very alien to him. Perhaps it had even been stupid.

He was almost in a panic to leave.

He looked around, briefly, to see if de Tormo was lurking in the shadows, but the priest remained missing. Dane continued out into the snowy church yard, passing by a man wrapped in a heavy, white woolen cloak who was heading into the church. He brushed the man because the snowy path kept them from moving too far out of the shoveled path of travel, but the man didn't waver. He merely lifted a hand as if to apologize for the brush. Dane also lifted a hand, simply to be polite, and continued on his way.

The land was settling in for the coming night, and everything was becoming quite dark now. The Shrewsbury escort had begun to light torches to see their way through the coming night, since it would be dark by the time they reached Deverill. Dane's boots crunched on the snowy path and he could see Grier as she stuck her head outside of the window again, now looking up at the night sky. As Dane walked past the front of his escort, he signaled the men to begin pulling out. Horses began to move forward as Dane went straight to the cab.

"We should be to Deverill shortly," he said. "Bundle up, sweetheart. The air is getting colder."

Grier watched him as he moved to collect his horse, which was standing right next to the cab with a soldier holding the reins.

"Did you find Father de Tormo?" she asked.

He nodded. "I did. He will come to Deverill tomorrow, so you shall meet him then."

As Dane mounted up, Grier turned her attention back to the sky. "I look forward to it," she said. "Did you notice what a beautiful night it is tonight?"

Dane was gathering his reins. "Probably not," he said. "But I did notice the clouds off to the east. It looks as if we may have snowfall for Christmas."

Grier could see the clouds, too, but her attention was on the clear sky above. "That would be nice," she said. Then, she pointed. "Look at that star, Dane. Have you ever seen anything so bright and shining?"

Dane glanced up as he moved his horse forward. Almost directly above them was a very bright star with a backdrop of deep blue sky. There were other stars around it, and the sky was rather brilliant with them, but that star in particular was quite bright.

"Lovely," he said, returning his attention to his wife as the cab began to move. "It seems appropriate, since this is Christmas Eve. Didn't the Magi follow a bright star to Bethlehem where the Christ Child was born?"

Grier nodded, her gaze on the sky for a few moments longer before settling back in the cab. "Indeed," she said. "They followed it to a stable where our Lord lay in a manger."

"Must have been scratchy."

"Dane!"

He grinned. "Sorry," he said, turning to wave a big arm at the escort behind him, men who were cold and a little slower to move. "But when you think about it, that must have been very stinky and uncomfortable."

She frowned at him. "That is sacrilegious!"

He was trying not to laugh. "It is realistic."

"Our Blessed Mother had no other choice but to give birth in a stable and you will not judge her for it."

Dane shook his head. "Never," he said. "One has to do what is necessary, I suppose."

That only brought a long look from his wife, who did not appreciate his sense of humor. Dane wouldn't have thought anything of it had he not remembered that not a few minutes before, he'd been begging God to heal his father. Perhaps God didn't appreciate his humor, either.

Casting a rather sheepish look heavenward, Dane hoped his heartfelt prayers weren't just negated by his humor. As he said, his faith wasn't particularly strong, but his love for his father was.

Musty mangers aside, he hoped God understood that.

PART TWO:
HOME

Deverill Castle

DANE HAD BEEN right; Grier had never seen so many people all from the same family.

Deverill Castle was a behemoth of a structure, with massive sand-colored walls, an enormous bailey, a great hall situated in the bailey, and then another smaller hall inside the keep itself.

It was inside this smaller hall that everyone from the de Russe family was gathered. When Dane and Grier arrived, they were accosted by men and women that Grier didn't even know. Everyone wanted to hug her and kiss her cheeks, and she smiled rather fearfully as strangers embraced her. Having no siblings of her own, and no family members, to be embraced by such a large family was somewhat intimidating at first.

But she knew she could come to like it.

The first person she saw was Trenton de Russe, a mountain of a man with a grin on his face as he kissed her cheek. Trenton introduced her to his wife, Lysabel, a lovely woman with blue eyes and a sweet face. She was carrying their baby son, Rafael, and Grier fawned over the infant as Trenton stood by proudly. But Trenton and Lysabel were pushed aside by another de Russe brother, Cort, a god of a man with a quick wit, followed by Boden, whom Grier already knew from his time serving her husband at Shrewsbury. He greeted her like a long-lost sister.

Next was another de Russe brother, Matthieu, who didn't look like the rest of the brothers too much. His hair was copper, his eyes green. He introduced his four boys, all young men who had little interest in a new aunt. The next two de Russe siblings were Gage and Gilliana; Grier had met Gage before, about a year ago when Gaston and his sons had come to Shrewsbury, but she'd never met Gilliana, the youngest de Russe child. Gilliana was a lush beauty with auburn hair and green eyes, and according to Gage and Boden, had suitors lined up from London to Cornwall. But she was quite sweet and Grier liked her immediately.

Just as she was warming to their conversation, it was cut short by the oldest sisters, twins Adeliza and Arica. They were identical copies of one another with eleven children clamoring at their feet. They were both quite lovely, and very kind, and Grier was pulled into their orbit, with one on each side, and she could hardly pull away. She cast Dane a rather helpless glance as the sisters closed in around her, including Gilliana, and they all went to sit over near the blazing hearth.

Dane stood with Trenton as the women seemed to cluster over near the hearth where the children were playing and running around, teasing each other. Even Lysabel went to sit with them, handing her son over to Grier, who took the baby with delight. Dane had to smile at his wife as she played with the toothless infant.

"You must be very proud," he said to Trenton. "You have a fine son."

Trenton wasn't humble about it in the least. "He is big and smart," he said. "Already he can sit up on his own and I swear to you that he is trying to talk. At only six months of age!"

Dane laughed softly at his serious and sometimes deadly brother; he never thought he'd see the day when the man would dote on an infant.

"Watch out when he does," he said. "Already, I can see that he rules your house and hold so when he can finally give orders, you will find yourself subservient to an infant."

Trenton shrugged. "I do not care," he said. "I am happy to play the fool for my son."

Dane simply nodded. "I am sure I will say that as well come the spring when mine is born."

Trenton looked at him in surprise. "Grier is with child?"

Dane nodded. "We have come to surprise Father with it."

Trenton laughed with joy, slapping his brother on the

shoulder. "He will be thrilled," he said. "So will Mother. Congratulations, old man. Considering we are the oldest of the de Russe siblings, it is about time we start having sons of our own."

Dane chuckled. "We are also the most accomplished and seasoned of the siblings."

"Indeed, we are."

"The rest of them cannot hold a candle to us."

"Well said. We are kings."

Dane began to laugh, followed by Trenton. They snorted and laughed at each other, so very happy to be in each other's company again. Their parents had married when Trenton was nine years of age, and Dane was eight, and they'd spent their entire lives together, fostering and training together. It went against the natural order for them to be apart but, unfortunately, it was necessary at this point in their lives. Therefore, spending time together, especially at the holidays, was particularly precious.

"Where *is* Mother, by the way?" Dane asked as the laughter died down. "I thought she would be here to greet us."

Trenton's smile faded, as well. "She will be," he said. "Father has not been eating, so she is up in their chamber trying to entice him into taking some nourishment. I am sure she will be down shortly."

Father has not been eating.

That killed Dane's mood immediately. He was thinking heavily on heading up to his parents' chamber when a crash distracted him and everyone else in the room. He turned to see Boden and Gage on the floor of the hall, having wrestled themselves right onto a bench that broke beneath their weight. As the two of them went at it, with Cort and Matthieu standing over them, Dane shook his head.

"Thank God Willie isn't here," he said. "Where are the Wellesbournes, anyway? I thought they would be here."

William Wellesbourne, or Willie as he was called, was the rambunctious youngest son of the House of Wellesbourne, family to the House of de Russe. The patriarchs, Gaston and Matthew Wellesbourne, had been friends for decades, closer than brothers, and Trenton had even married Matthew's eldest daughter in Lysabel.

Therefore, when there was any great de Russe gathering, it was a sure bet that the House of Wellesbourne would be there. But not tonight, and Dane was rather surprised by it.

"They should be here in a day or two," Trenton said. "Matt has caught a chill that has settled in his chest, and Aunt Alix will not let him travel until he is well again. Given Father's condition, neither Aunt Alix or Mother wanted to chance Matt giving Father whatever infection he has."

"I am sorry to hear that," Dane said. "I cannot recall a Christmas we have not spent with Uncle Matt. I sent Willie home to ride escort with his father to Deverill for the holidays, you know."

William served Dane at Shrewsbury and in spite of his boisterous nature, he was a fine knight whom Dane depended on. Matthew had sent his wild son north to serve Dane and hopefully grow up in the process, and it had worked for the most part. At least, it had worked until he came within range of Boden and Gage, and then he turned into a naughty seven-year-old child again.

But it was all part of his charm.

"Willie would do well to remain at Wellesbourne Castle with his father for now," Trenton said. "How has he been at Shrewsbury?"

"He has moments when I want to take a club to him. Then he has other moments when he is fine, reasonable, and strong." Dane sighed as he watched Boden and Gage roll around on the ground, fighting. "Part of me hopes Willie, much like Boden and Gage, never loses his wild streak. It makes family reunions so much more interesting."

Trenton snorted. "God," he groaned. "Remember when it was just us? Remember when things were peaceful and quiet before our parents decided to have wild animals as children?"

Dane looked at him as if he'd lost his mind. "We were never peaceful and quiet, Trenton," he said. "Remember when we were fostering at Oxford and we stole an old nag to ride north to Yorkshire? That was *not* a peaceful nor a quiet venture."

Trenton couldn't stop laughing. "Remember the traveler we stole from?" he asked. "I stole the rabbit he was cooking, and you stole his pants so he could not run after us. Mother tried to beat us for it when she found out."

Dane was chuckling. "Ungrateful wench. We did it to help her."

"She did not appreciate our efforts."

"Father did."

The laughter faded almost immediately. It was difficult to speak of Gaston and not feel a stab of sorrow, for either of them. Dane finally spoke on the subject that had been weighing on him so heavily, fearful to speak of it as if even mentioning the subject somehow made it far more real.

"I stopped at St. Denys on the way into town," he said. "I saw Father de Tormo. He says that Father hasn't been to church in quite some time."

Trenton nodded, but it was a gesture made with a heavy heart. "That is true," he said. "De Tormo has been coming to Deverill for the past several months so Father does not have to exert himself."

Dane sighed. "He is not going to live much longer, is he?"

Trenton didn't say anything for a moment. When Dane turned to look at him, he was blinking rapidly, as if blinking back the tears.

"It is possible," he finally said. "I cannot even bring myself to think on it. I see him every day, Dane. Now that I command his armies, I am with my father every single day and I have seen a steady decline over the months. His hair is grayer, his footsteps slower... I honestly do not know how much time he has left, but it is not much. How long can you remain here at Deverill?"

Dane shrugged. "As long as I wish, I suppose," he said. "I have left my second in command, Dastan du Reims, in charge of Shrewsbury. You met Dastan when you visited last year."

Trenton nodded. "I did," he said. "A competent man."

"One of the best," Dane said. "I feel confident leaving him in command while I spend time here with Father. Truthfully, I am afraid to leave now, afraid that I will never see him alive again."

Trenton grunted. "That is a very real fear, with all of us." He suddenly caught a glimpse of something behind Dane. "Ah. Mother is here."

They both turned to see Remington de Russe emerging from the stairwell that led to the upper floors of the keep. A gorgeous woman with copper curls pinned at the nape of her neck, she looked far younger than her years. Seeing Dane, her first born, had her rushing in his direction with her arms open. The pair came together in a fierce hug.

"Dane," Remington said with satisfaction. "You have finally arrived. I have been waiting all week for you to come, and now you are finally here. It is so good to see you."

Dane kissed his mother's soft cheek, pulling back to look into her sea-colored eyes. It was the face he'd always known, perhaps a little older, a little more lined, but no less beautiful. Dane knew he had the most beautiful mother in all of England.

"It is good to see you, too," he said with satisfaction. "You are looking well."

Remington smiled broadly. "As are you, my son, the duke," she said, her gaze drifting over him as if reacquainting herself with the little boy she'd known, the man he'd now become. "I am so proud of you, Dane. You cannot know how full my heart is. The whole family is so very happy and thrilled for you."

Dane smiled. "I've not seen you since it all happened," he said. "It seems like so long ago, but it has only been two years now. I have written to you since then but, somehow, it is not the same to write. It has been ages since we have had a nice, long talk."

Remington's smile faded as she patted her son on his stubbled cheek. "It has," she said. "And you are correct; it is not the same for your father to come and tell me of your life at Shrewsbury, and it is not the same for Trenton to tell me nearly the same thing. I have wanted to go north to visit you, many times, but your father does not wish for me to travel without him, and he cannot travel these days. So... I was waiting for you to come to Deverill to tell you how proud I am of you and how much I love you."

Dane kissed her hands, feeling emotional about the reunion with his beloved mother. Her pride meant everything to him, and he didn't realize until this very moment how much he'd missed her. Until Gaston had come into her life those years ago, it had always been just Dane and his mother for the most part, but her sisters had also been part of that equation. They had lived together at Mt. Holyoak Castle in Yorkshire, a property that still belonged to Gaston, but one Dane hadn't seen in years. He had been born there. But it wasn't his home.

Deverill was.

"I love you, too," he said. "I have missed you so much. I have missed Father, too. Is… is he awake that I might at least greet him?"

Remington tried to smile but she couldn't quite manage it. "He has gone to sleep," she said. "The physic has given him poppy powder for the pain in his throat, and it always makes him sleep. You will see him in the morning. I know he wants to see you very much."

Looking into her eyes, Dane could see the agony there. Gaston was her whole world. Certainly, the woman had children and grandchildren, but those did not replace a husband, and Gaston and Remington were closer than most. They had a relationship that men could only dream of, and as worried as Dane was about his father's health, he knew his mother was far more worried. Dane couldn't help feeling even more worried as he looked at her.

"Trenton says he is not eating these days," he said. "*How* is he, Mother? Please be truthful."

Remington swallowed hard; Dane saw it. Then, she forced a smile and reached out to Trenton, who was still standing next to Dane. She held both of their hands, her gaze moving back and forth between them.

"When I met your father, God only knows, I was terrified of him," she said. "Do you recall, Dane? The first time you met him was at the base of Mt. Holyoak Castle, when he was returning from a trip. I do not even recall what it was. But I do recall the look on your face when you first saw him. Do you?"

Dane nodded, a smile playing on his lips even though there was a lump in his throat. "I do," he said hoarsely. "I had never seen such a frightening man."

Remington's smile grew. "Your aunts were terrified of him, also," she said. "I cannot count the times your Aunt Jasmine fainted at the sight of him and your Aunt Skye would cower. Only Aunt Rory showed no fear of him. Whether or not that was smart, I do not know, but she showed no fear. Gaston always respected her for that, although he would not admit it. Her death those years ago in the ambush that took her life hit him harder than he cared to realize, almost as hard as Arik's death hit him."

Dane remembered that incident, years ago, when his sixteen-year-old aunt, Rory, was caught in an ambush perpetrated by Gaston's enemies. Also killed in the ambush had been Gaston's dear friend and right-hand man, Arik Helgeson. Dane's sister, Arica, had been named for the tall Northman as a way of keeping his memory alive.

"I remember," Dane said. "That was a very terrible time for us all."

Remington nodded, her smile fading as she thought on

her long-dead sister with the flaming red hair.

"Please do not tell your father what I am about to tell you," she said as her eyes began to glimmer with tears. "I can tell the two of you, but I would not tell him because I do not want him to fret. I know your father will die before I will. I know he will leave me behind. But the only thing that gives me comfort is knowing that Rory and Arik will be waiting for him when he crosses over. He will close his eyes and go to sleep, and when he awakens, Rory and Arik will be there to greet him, keeping him company until I can join him. Although I do not want to lose him, at least I know he will not be alone. I am at peace because of it, and when Gaston takes his last breath, he will hear my voice in his ear, telling him that he has my permission to go."

Tears spilled over in Dane's eyes and he lowered his head, quickly wiping them away. Trenton was less discreet; he didn't even lower his head. He simply wiped at his eyes. But Remington wasn't crying. She watched her eldest boys, two of the most powerful men in the realm. But to her, they would always be those little boys who liked to get into trouble. And they were boys who loved their father very much.

Taking a deep breath to fight off the solemn mood, Remington squeezed Trenton's hand and kissed Dane on the cheek.

"Now," she said firmly. "Let us not reflect on sorrow this night. All of my children are here and I want to rejoice. And your wife, Dane? I've not even met the lovely Grier yet. I am so anxious to know her."

Dane forced a smile, but it was difficult. His mother's words had him shaken but he fought it. Taking her by the hand, he led her over to the hearth where the women and children were gathered, and where Grier still had Trenton's baby in her lap. But a touch to the shoulder from Dane caused Grier to look up, seeing a woman at his side who looked a good deal like him.

And with that, Grier handed the baby back to Lysabel and met her mother-in-law for the very first time. She was greeted sweetly and gently, and already, there was love and approval in the air. Within two minutes, Grier felt as if she'd known Remington all her life.

It was magic.

While Grier and Dane and Remington became acquainted, and the de Russe family gathered in the hall for a night of celebration and reflection, a visitor in an off-white cloak made his way into the gatehouse of Deverill.

He'd come all the way from the village, walking in the snow. Once he entered the gatehouse, he was directed by the sentries to the great hall where other travelers had stopped to wait out the freezing weather. Deverill never turned away travelers in search of shelter, and especially not on Christmas Eve, so the man thanked the guards at the gatehouse and made his way to the great hall to wait out the storm that was gathering overhead.

At least, that was what the guards at the gatehouse thought.

Because of his pale cloak against the snowy bailey, the guards failed to see the man as he moved for the keep, which was open this time of night as servants moved through not only the front entrance, but also through the smaller rear entrance, which would be left open most of the night so the servants and guards could come in out of the bad weather.

The visitor in the white cloak moved easily towards the small rear entrance to the keep, disappearing before anyone ever saw him.

Overhead, the clouds began to gather, but the bright and shining star remained strong.

PART THREE:
THE STRANGER

G ASTON WASN'T ASLEEP.

He should have been, and he knew his wife had give him a poppy powder prescribed by the physic, but he was fighting it. He knew that Dane had arrived because he could see the remnants of the Shrewsbury escort in the bailey down below. That was both the curse and the advantage of having windows that faced out over the bailey; he could see everything that was going on.

And that had him restless.

Even so, he was exhausted to the bone, which was ironic consider he didn't do anything these days. He stayed to his chamber, he drank the warm milk his wife gave him and ate the pea soup with bits of pork fat in it that he liked. He pretended to be more invalid than he really was because it kept Remington with him longer, tending to his every need, and then he felt guilty because he could see the grave concern in her eyes.

But the truth was that he was concerned, too.

Whatever was tearing up his throat had moved into his lungs; he could feel it. He'd very nearly lost his voice and there were times when he coughed so hard that blood came up. The physic told him that was because the cancer had moved into his lungs, but Gaston swore the physic to secrecy on that. He didn't want Remington knowing that because she had enough to worry over. Sometime soon, he was going to leave her with only his memory to keep her warm, and that was tearing him apart. He didn't want to leave her and, these days, she had enough to worry over.

Which was why he didn't go running downstairs to see Dane. As if he could actually run. He hadn't run in months; probably years. He knew the moment he went to the hall, Remington would be stricken with worry, and he didn't want to cause her any undue grief. But he very much wanted to see Dane, and his other children, and his grandchildren.

There were times when Remington would forbid the grandchildren entry into his chamber because they would jump all over his bed, but he would send Trenton to sneak them up the servant's stairs when Remington was occupied elsewhere. Trenton had become his cohort in crime, but it had brought the two of them even closer than ever. His eldest son, who he'd been intermittently estranged from until last year, had become his closest friend.

He was grateful for small mercies.

So, Gaston stood at the window, watching the clouds

gather overhead as a snowstorm threatened. It was Christmas Eve and, given his health, he wondered if it would be the last one he ever saw. That thought caused him to summon his courage about going down to the hall; he wanted to spend all the time he could with his family, even if moving and talking was a great labor for him. He didn't want to miss anything. Remington would fuss at him, but he hoped she would understand why he was exerting himself.

As he began to look around for his heavy robe to protect against the cold drafts of the castle, there was a gentle knock at the door.

"Come," Gaston rasped.

The door creaked open and timid footsteps entered. Gaston had just found his robe, turning around to see a stranger enter his chamber. He eyed the man as he swung his robe over his shoulders.

"Who are you?" he asked.

The man took another step into the chamber and closed the door. He was very tall, sinewy, with blond hair and pale blue eyes. He was quite pale, in fact, made more pale by the white-woolen cloak he wore.

"My name is Raphael," he said. "Dane has sent me. He says that you are ill, great lord."

Gaston grunted. "Raphael," he repeated. "I have a grandson by that name. You are a physic, you say? Did Dane bring you with him from Shrewsbury? Never mind. The last thing I need is another physic."

Raphael took another step, coming nearer to the enormous bed as Gaston fussed with his robe. "Dane is quite worried for you," he said, his voice soft and higher-pitched. "He says that you are ill."

Gaston eyed him before opening his mouth to speak, but he was overcome by a series of heavy coughs which shook his big body. He was forced to grab for a handkerchief, coughing into it because blood was coming up. The coughing was so violent that he ended up plopping onto the bed until the coughing died off. By that time, Raphael had come around the corner of the bed and was standing over him.

"I suspect you have been ill for some time," he said quietly. "You were ill before you even told your wife and family because you did not wish to worry them."

Gaston took a deep breath, looking at the bloodied handkerchief before putting it on the table next to the bed.

"Did Dane tell you that?" he asked, raspy.

Raphael smiled faintly. "Nay," he said. "He did not have to. You are a selfless man when it comes to your family."

Gaston simply lifted his eyebrows as if to agree. The coughing fit had left him weak. "Well," he said after a moment. "I suppose I cannot turn you away if Dane has brought you all the way from Shrewsbury. If you are to give me a potion, then get on with it. But I will tell you that there is nothing you can give me that the best physics in London have not already tried."

Rafael flipped his cloak back, revealing unbleached woolen breeches and a heavy tunic, and a small satchel in his hand that was made from an unfamiliar material. It glistened weakly in the light, but Gaston wasn't really looking at it. He was looking at the tall, graceful man as he became somewhat curious about him.

"When Dane sent me a missive telling me that he would be here for Christmas, he did not mention bringing a physic with him," he said.

Raphael opened his satchel and began rummaging around. "Mayhap, he'd not yet decided I was needed," he said. "Mayhap, he did not wish to upset you."

"We are speaking of Dane," Gaston reminded him. "He could not upset me if he tried."

Raphael was pulling something out of his satchel that Gaston couldn't quite see. "He spoke of a man with the reputation as the Dark One," he said. "He also spoke of a man who saved him and his mother from a man who was truly wicked."

Gaston looked up at him, somewhat surprised as the subject veered away from his health and onto his reputation and past.

"He told you about Stoneley?" he asked.

"Aye."

"Why should he do that?"

Raphael was pouring something into a small cup; Gaston could hear the liquid. "I suppose he wanted to explain what kind of man you were and what you meant to him."

Gaston's gaze lingered on him a moment before turning away. "What he spoke of was long ago," he muttered. "Dane's father by blood and the Dark One... that was long ago."

"You sound as if you are not proud of your past."

Gaston grunted. "I have done nothing in my life that I have regretted," he said. "Mayhap that is not repentant enough, for all men sin, and I am certain I have done my share of it. But it does not matter now. One cannot change the past."

Raphael paused a moment before turning to him. "In your case, I am not sure you should want to," he said. "I have heard the story of your greatness from others. Long ago, you saved innocent women and a child from a man who was possessed by a demon. There is much wickedness in this world, great lord. You thought you had seen all of it until you came to a fortress in Yorkshire where the inhabitants lived in fear of a monster. It was you who saved them. You were their angel of mercy."

Gaston shrugged. "Mayhap to Dane, I was."

Raphael turned to him, cup in hand. "It was not Dane who told me that."

Gaston looked at him with interest. "Who told you?"

"A man who was there."

"*Who*?"

"One named de Tormo."

Gaston's brow furrowed. "De Tormo?" he repeated. "Which de Tormo? If you refer to the priest at St. Denys, he was not there, but his older brother… he was, indeed, there. He is a man I owe a great deal to, but you are too young to have known him."

"I am older than you think."

Gaston looked at him rather doubtfully. "How old are you?"

Raphael extended the cup, his pale eyes glimmering. "Drink this, great lord."

He completely avoided answering the question and Gaston found himself with a cup in his face. He eyed it.

"What is it?" he asked.

"It is blessed and pure. It will not harm you, I promise."

Gaston sighed heavily before reaching up to take the cup, peering at the contents. "I suppose it cannot hurt me," he said in resignation. "One more potion is not going to make a difference."

With that, he tossed it back, smacking his lips as he handed the cup back to Raphael. But then, he looked at the man rather strangely.

"That was water," he said.

Raphael nodded. "It is, indeed," he said. "It is holy water."

"You had me drink holy water?"

"As you said, it cannot hurt you."

He had a point. Gaston cleared his throat, coughing a little, and thinking about trying to make it down to the hall again.

"You can tell Dane I took your potion," he said. "For coming all the way to Deverill from Shrewsbury, I thank you."

Raphael grinned. "I have come much farther than that."

Gaston wasn't sure what he meant by that statement but he didn't ask. He was more concerned with going down to the hall but, suddenly, he began to feel rather sleepy, as if the poppy powder his wife had given him had just begun to take effect. Or perhaps it was all of the coughing. Whatever the case, he was beginning to feel quite tired.

"For your effort, I thank you," he said again. "You will forgive me for not showing you out, but I find that I am feeling rather weary."

He started to remove his heavy robe and Raphael stepped forward, helping him pull it off. Gaston's movements were slow, lethargic.

Old.

It was clear from Raphael's expression that he felt pity for the man. There was great compassion in his actions.

"I will go. But before I do, I must tell you something," he said. "In spite of the earlier life you lived, as a knight bent on death and destruction, your fears on whether or not you shall ascend to heaven are for naught. You have feared that, have you not?"

Gaston looked at him as if confused by the question. "Why should you ask that?"

"Is it true?"

Gaston paused. He saw no reason to deny the obvious; it was of little matter, even to speak of it to this perceptive stranger.

"I think that is something all men fear, whether or not they shall go to heaven when they die."

Raphael smiled at his honesty. "You redeemed yourself the moment you fought to save your wife and her son and her sisters from a man who was the embodiment of evil," he said. "You did not know it then, but you were filled with the power of the archangels during that time. Most men would have left them to their fates, and although your actions at first were driven by lust, the love that consumed your heart for Remington and Dane cleansed you of all sin because it was pure. Pure of intent, pure of composition. Good overcame sin, you see. God could see into your heart, and it had been redeemed. You needn't worry whether or not you shall ascend to heaven; there is a place for you there, great lord. Do not be troubled."

Gaston simply shook his head, staring at the man with wide eyes. "How could you know that?" he asked, awed. "How could you know all of that? *Who* told you?"

Raphael's smile grew. "I told you," he said. "De Tormo has pleaded on your behalf to Our Lord but, in the end, he did not need to. When you are ready to join us, we shall be waiting for you. But it shall not be tonight."

Gaston still didn't understand. "Father Otho de Tormo died many years ago," he said. "In his death, he helped me more than he ever did in life. Did you know him?"

Raphael nodded. "I do."

"You *do*?"

Raphael bent over, pushing Gaston onto his back on the big bed. There was something intense about his gaze, but his movements were gentle. It was clear that he was a caring and considerate individual. As he pulled the coverlet over Gaston, he spoke.

"Sometimes, men do not always live a life they are proud of," he said. "You, great lord, have lived a life to be proud of, in all ways. Dane has said you are a man of principles. He has spoken of his great love for you, and of your family's great love for you. If I knew nothing else about you, knowing of your family's powerful love for you would tell me everything I needed to know. Fear not for the past, or of the reputation as the Dark One. Men change, as you have. You have a legacy to be proud of."

Gaston was looking up at the man. Odd how a stranger's words should impact him so, but the man seemed to know a great deal about him. For most, that would have been off-putting, but for Gaston, he felt strangely kindred with the man.

"Did Otho tell you all of this?" he finally asked.

Raphael smiled. "He did," he said. "But there have been others, men who have known you over the years. Great lord, you have been ill for some time, and pain wracks your body, and that is a sign that God is near. Tell me something; if you could ask one thing of God, what would it be?"

Gaston didn't know why he considered the question seriously. He really didn't. He thought this physic was a little too religious for his taste, but there was something about the man that made him unable to look away. Perhaps he was tired; perhaps he was weak. Whatever the case, he found himself responding to the question.

"I do not want to leave my family," he said, his eyes welling with tears he fought to keep away. "I grew up lonely. I never had a family until I met Remington, and now… now, if wealth was measured by love, I am the richest man in the world. I have strong sons and beautiful daughters, and many grandchildren. I have a life that men dream of. What would I ask of God? That I could known good health again. I cannot stand my wife and children seeing me this way. I feel old and feeble, and that is no way for a warrior to feel. Once, I was the strongest knight in the realm. I want to feel that way again. That is what I would ask of God."

Raphael nodded in understanding. "As I suspected," he said. "You would not ask for wealth or glory, only health."

"A man's health is more valuable than all the gold or glory in England."

Raphael smiled. "All men should be as wise as you, great lord," he said. "Mayhap, that which you ask for shall be yours."

"Only if a miracle occurs."

Raphael simply moved away from the bed and back to his

satchel. "Sleep, now," he said. "I have done what I was sent to do."

Gaston watched the man tie off his satchel and collect it under his arm. His gaze then drifted to the windows, which had the oil cloths peeled back. He could see a light dusting of snow beginning to fall.

"It is this night when men feel closest to God," Gaston muttered, his eyes heavy-lidded now. "Someone told me once that it is on Christmas Eve when angels walk the earth because it was on this very night that the angel appeared to the shepherds in the field to tell them of the birth of the Christ Child. I saw such a star tonight, in fact. I wonder if it is a sign that an angel has appeared somewhere."

Raphael pulled his cloak around him, his gaze lingering on Gaston. "Would you believe me if I told you that one has?"

Gaston's lips twitched with a smile but, by then, sleep had claimed him. He could not reply.

Pulling his cloak more tightly about him, Raphael quit the chamber and slipped down the servant's stairs, going out the way he'd come. Out into the snowy night, he headed for the gatehouse, slipping out just as the sentries were sealing it up for the night. They saw the man go and called to him to return, but he waved them off, heading into the flurried darkness.

As he disappeared into the night, the bright and shining star overhead, which had been the only thing visible as the snow clouds rolled in, began to fade away. More clouds covered it, and the light gradually went away, a phenomenon not unnoticed by the sentries at the gatehouse. They, too, had noticed that brilliant star that had appeared at dusk. But now, it was obscured by the clouds.

Or, so they thought.

It was a star they would talk about in years to come, but a star they would never see again.

It was a star that had served its purpose.

PART FOUR:
THE BEST CHRISTMAS OF ALL

I T WAS A cold, bright, and fresh morning, and Dane had just received a snowball on the side of the head, launched with precision by Cort, who was now running for his life as Dane charged after him. Everyone was screaming and laughing as Dane tackled Cort, who slipped on the ice, and the two of them went plowing into a snowdrift.

But Dane wasn't alone. When next he realized, children were piling on top of him and on top of Cort, egged on by Trenton and Matthieu. It was Matthieu's four boys who were the first ones to pile on, followed by an assortment of other children. Dane started laughing, so hard that he could barely breathe, but he managed to grab a fistful of show and rub it into Cort's face.

It was bedlam.

Somehow, Dane made it out of the pile of men and children, wet and covered with snow, but he hardly cared. Christmas morn had dawned bright and beautiful after a storm overnight, and it was a winter wonderland for everyone to play in. Not surprisingly, the first ones out into the snow had been Boden and Gage, and they'd awakened the entire keep by pounding on doors, awakening the children, announcing that it was Christmas morn.

They had taken their lives in their hands doing so.

Matthieu's sons had been the first ones to join their uncles, joined by more children as the parents couldn't keep them still. All eleven of Adeliza and Arica's children emerged, bundled up and ready for the morning, and it was Boden and Gage who herded the children down into the bailey where great piles of fresh snow awaited. Screaming, happy children filled the morning.

Trenton brought his two daughters down soon enough, and Brencis and Cynethryn joined in the fun. They were Lysabel's daughters from her first marriage, but Trenton had adopted them when he married their mother, and he loved them as if they were his own blood. Lysabel remained in their chamber, feeding their son, but Dane and Grier joined the chaos in the bailey, with Grier staying far out of the way as the brothers de Russe lobbed snowballs at each other.

Unfortunately for Grier, Gage tried to use her as a human shield against her husband, which Dane didn't take kindly to. As he was demanding Gage release his wife, Trenton came up behind his youngest brother and smashed snow down the back of his coat. Howling, Gage released Grier, who laughingly ran to the safety of her husband as Trenton further punished Gage by dragging the man over to a snowdrift and pushing him into it. It was the older brothers against the younger brothers as the balance of power shifted.

Last to join the fray were Remington and her youngest daughter, Gilliana. Bundled up in furs, they stood on the stoop of the keep entry, watching the madness. Gilliana didn't want to get cold and wet, but she was pulled away by her nieces and had no choice but to play in the snow. Seeing his mother standing alone on the steps, Dane went to join her.

"Good morn to you, Mother," he said, kissing her cheek. "A happy and chaotic Christmas to you."

Remington touched her boy on the cheek. "A happy Christmas to you as well," she said. "Did you sleep well?"

Dane nodded, watching Grier as Brencis and Cynethryn pulled her out into the snow, trying to convince her to help them build a snow fortress. "I did," he said. "Shrewsbury Castle may belong to me, but Deverill is home. I feel as if this is where I truly belong."

Remington smiled. "It *is* where you truly belong," she said. "Is Grier happy? Did she sleep well?"

Dane was looking at his wife as she began to help her nieces make a snow fort. "She did," he said. "Which is normal for her. She can sleep anywhere, any time of day. Being with child has made her exhausted."

Remington's eyes flew open wide as she looked to her son in shock. "A baby?" she gasped. Then, she threw her arms around her son. "Dane, I am so thrilled for you! What a glorious Christmas gift!"

Dane hugged his mother. "We were going to surprise Father with it, but I am finding it increasingly difficult not to tell everyone before I tell him," he said. As his mother released him, he gazed into her eyes. "I have not discussed this with Grier yet, but I am sure she will agree with me. Regardless if the child is male or female, I would like to name my firstborn Rory, after Aunt Rory. You will recall, she was my playmate for many years. I miss the woman with the bright red hair who would do anything I asked of her, up to and including baiting hooks or climbing trees. I have never told you how much I have missed her because I never wanted to add to your sorrow, but I have missed her every single day. I would like to honor her by naming my child after her."

Remington's breath caught in her throat and, immediately, she was teary-eyed. "I think that would be wonderful," she said, a lump in her throat. "She loved you so much, Dane. I know she would be so very touched that you would name your child after her."

Dane smiled weakly. "Good," he said. "As I said, I've not mentioned it to Grier, but I am sure she will agree."

Remington held his hand tightly as they spent a moment thinking of Rory, a memory to bring the woman alive after all these years. Trenton, who hadn't really known Rory, had been listening in on the conversation, absorbing the past sorrows. He knew Arik, of course, his father's tall and blond friend, not unlike Matthew Wellesbourne. His father was close to both men. But Arik was a Viking, the son of Northmen, and that had seemed both frightening and exotic to Trenton as a young man.

All shadows of the past, things and people he remembered as a child. But those memories all revolved around his father, a man who was increasingly on Trenton's mind as the morning went on.

"Mayhap, Dane and I should go and wake Father," he said to Remington. "Mayhap we can help him dress and bring him down to the bailey to watch his grandchildren play. You know that he can probably already hear them."

He was pointing upward, to the chambers above them where Gaston was, and Remington glanced upward. She knew that Trenton was right. But there was hesitation in her manner.

"I will go," she said. "Trenton, Dane… you know your father does not like you to see him in his weakened state. At least let me get him dressed. Give him the dignity of facing you from a chair, or sitting up in bed, not laying on his back like an invalid. I know you mean well, but…"

She was cut off when Brencis, Trenton's youngest daughter, approached. The child was wailing, rubbing at her eyes, as she headed straight for Trenton, who bent down to pick her up.

"Here, here," he said gently, surprising from a man of his size and fierceness. "Why do you weep?"

Brencis' heart was broken. "I-I want to play with Bryant and Braxton and Etienne," she sobbed, pointing to her older cousins. "But they will not let me!"

Trenton fought off a grin as he looked to his mother. "Excuse me," he said quietly. "I have some boys to see."

Remington grinned as she waved him on, watching him lumber out to a group of nephews who were lobbing snowballs that had rocks in them. One of the boys already had a welt on his head. Seeing Uncle Trenton approach caused all activity to cease because the de Russe nephews had a healthy respect for their very big uncle, and it was soon clear that Brencis would be allowed to join their play, sans the rocks. Dane laughed softly at the sight.

"I never thought I would see the day when a young girl had complete power over Trenton," he said.

Remington snorted. "Wait until Rory is born," she said. "If it is a girl, I will remind you of this when you go running to her with every little cry she makes."

Dane shook his head. "Not me," he said firmly, pretending it wasn't true. "Here, let us go and say good morn to Grier. You can tell her how happy you are about our coming child."

Clutching her son's arm, Remington beamed as she headed out into the snow, where one of her cheeky grandchildren decided to throw a snowball at her. That brought Dane on the run, and he grabbed Adeliza's daughter, Marguerite, who reminded him a good deal of Rory. She was bold and brassy and redheaded. As he picked her up and tickled her to punish her, the sentries at the gate let up a cry.

As Dane set his niece to the ground, he could see a rider and donkey enter the compound, realizing almost immediately that it was Father de Tormo. As he'd promised yesterday, the priest was making an appearance at Deverill. He lifted a hand to the man, who waved in return. He was about to head in the priest's direction when he suddenly heard a collective gasp go up around him. Children began running towards the keep, and by the time Dane turned to see what was going on, he caught sight of his father standing on the stoop.

Gaston had finally made an appearance.

But it wasn't just any appearance. The man was bundled up in woolens, but he was moving differently. *Faster.* As the children ran at him, he bent down and scooped up two of them, kissing cold cheeks and greeting the ones who were clamoring at his feet. He hadn't picked up his grandchildren in months. As Dane stood there in shock, he could hear his mother gasp.

"My God," she hissed. "What is he doing?"

Remington began moving towards him, quickly, as Dane followed. In fact, all of the adults seemed to be moving for Gaston as the grandchildren began tugging on his hands, begging him to come out and play. Remington was the first one to her husband, her expression suggesting that she was panic-stricken with concern.

"Gaston?" she asked, trying to be gentle but not doing a very good job of it. "What... what are you doing out here, my love? How did you come down the stairs all on your own?"

Gaston looked at his wife with a hint of color in his cheeks that she hadn't seen since his illness had been diagnosed. And his expression... full of love and warmth and joy. It had been months, at the very least, since she'd seen that expression. He moved through the children gathered around him and reached out to pull Remington against him, planting a fairly alluring kiss on her lips.

"Good morn to you, angel," he said in a tone she hadn't heard from him in years. "I heard everyone out here and thought I would come and play."

A chorus went up among the children. *Play, play* they all cried. Adeliza and Arica were there, pulling the children away from Gaston. They were as confused as the rest of the adults as to why the man was on his feet. In fact, Boden and Gage were on either side of their father as if waiting for him to collapse, but he seemed as strong as a tree. *Healthy.* Remington was still staring at him, shock in her features.

"But..." she sputtered, reaching up to touch his face as if she couldn't quite believe what she was seeing. "You look... *well*, Gaston. How do you feel?"

Gaston grinned; he looked a little tired, perhaps a little elderly, but for the most part, he looked completely healthy. His dark hair, now mostly gone to gray, had been combed, and there was an energy to his movements that hadn't been seen from the man in ages.

"I feel remarkable," he said. "I woke up this morning feeling better than I have in quite some time."

"Father?" Dane was there, looking at the man with his mouth hanging open. "Are you sure you are feeling well? Mayhap, you should let Boden and Gage take you back inside so that you may rest."

Gaston looked to his blond son, a glimmer in his smoky gray eyes. "I do not need to rest," he said. "The physic you sent to me has done something no physic has been able to do. Whatever the man had me drink last night has worked wonders. My throat is still a bit sore, but no coughing. No blood. I woke up this morning feeling better than I have in a very long while."

Dane was vastly confused. "The physic *I* sent to you?"

Gaston nodded. "The one from Shrewsbury. The one dressed in white; tall, pale, and blond? Surely you know the man. He said you sent him."

Dane had no idea who he was talking about. "Father, I didn't bring a physic with me from Shrewsbury," he said with concern. "Who came to you and told you I had sent them?"

The children were tugging at Gaston, pulling at him, and it was increasingly difficult to resist. Adeliza and Arica couldn't keep them away, so they finally gave up because Gaston was going along with it.

"He said his name was Raphael," Gaston said. "He gave me something to drink. Holy water, he said, but it must have been much more than that. Whatever medicines he gave me, they have worked a miracle. It is the best Christmas gift you could have ever given me, Dane. To thank you doesn't seem quite enough."

With that, the lure of playing with his grandchildren took hold and he headed out with the group of them, still followed closely by Gage and Boden, still waiting for their father to collapse. But he didn't. He let himself be pelted by snowballs by eager little hands and it was the most glorious thing he could have hoped for. He was still old, that was true, but the illness that had been leeching away his life seemed, for a moment, to have faded away. Standing before them was the Gaston de Russe they all knew and loved, a man of strength and with a lust for life.

It was the most astonishing thing any of the adults had ever seen.

Trenton turned to Dane.

"*Who* is this physic he is speaking of?" he demanded softly. "Did someone come to him last night that we did not know about?"

Neither Dane nor Remington had any answers for him. "I only left him for a short while," Remington insisted. "When I came down to greet Dane. And you know that I did not stay very long. When I returned to his chamber, he was quite alone and asleep."

Dane was at a loss. Watching his father as the man played with his grandchildren was the most dumbfounding thing he'd ever seen. Nothing the man had said made any sense to him but, clearly, something had happened.

For a brief and wonderful moment, Gaston de Russe's health had returned.

He was the man they all remembered.

"A blessed Christmas, Lady de Russe."

Father de Tormo was walking up on the group, trying not to slip in the snow. He opened his mouth to say something more when he caught sight of Gaston standing in the center of a group of frolicking children. Eyes wide, he pointed to him.

"What... Sweet Mary, *what* is he doing?" he gasped. "I thought he could not leave his bed!"

Trenton and Dane were shaking their heads in unison, hardly able to grasp the sight. They reflected the priest's shock and then some.

"He says someone visited him last night and gave him a potion," Dane said. "He said the man identified himself as being sent by me, but I sent no one."

"God," Trenton groaned, hand to his face. "Is it possible he has gone mad? Is it possible that he has simply lost his mind?"

By this time, Cort had joined the group as they all stood there and watched Gaston with his grandchildren. Cort came up to his mother and put his arm around her shoulders.

"He's possessed," Cort said flatly. "He must be. Yesterday, he had not the strength to move but today, he is standing and playing? He is possessed, I say!"

Remington wasn't sure how to respond. She was so worried that she could hardly stand it, but Gaston didn't look like he was in any distress. In fact, this was the man she knew from years ago, the strong and healthy husband, and that realization brought tears to her eyes. Now that she was over the shock of his appearance, something was abundantly clear to her – something miraculous had, indeed, happened, and the warmth of an overwhelming feeling of faith washed over her like nothing she'd ever experienced before. Not a religious woman, it was something Remington had never felt before. Choked with emotion, she could barely speak.

"Nay," she breathed. "He is not possessed."

"But – *how*?" Cort demanded.

Remington could only shake her head. "You know I have struggled with my faith," she whispered. "My prayers have never been answered, so when your father became ill, I did not bother with prayer because I knew I would be ignored. But... but at this moment, I have never felt faith more strongly or purely in my life. Mayhap, I am living a dream. Mayhap, we are *all* living a dream for, certainly, this is what I see when I dream – I see Gaston as I remember him. I see him as he is meant to be. I do not care what has happened to him, or why he has suddenly regained his health, but I am not going to question it. Mayhap that is what is means to have faith and, today, I am full of it. Blindly full of it. I am going to enjoy every moment and be grateful for it."

With that, she went to her husband as he stood in the center of their grandchildren. When he saw her coming, he opened up an arm to her and she went to him, collapsing against him as he pulled her into an embrace.

It was enough to drive Dane and Trenton to tears.

"Is this really happening?" Dane finally asked, deeply moved. "God, I prayed for this moment. When I lit the candle yesterday at St. Denys, this is exactly what I prayed for. And that physic that my father spoke of? Was it possible that he dreamed the man, like some kind of miraculous healer?"

"Miraculous healer?" Cort repeated. He hadn't heard what Gaston had said about the situation, so this was new information to him. "He said he dreamed of a physic?"

Dane nodded. "He said someone came to him last night and told him that I had sent him, from Shrewsbury, presumably. But I sent no one from Shrewsbury."

Cort's gaze lingered on his brother a moment before returning his attention to his father. "Did he describe the man?" he asked.

"He said he was dressed in white, tall and blond." Dane suddenly paused as a thought occurred to him. "In fact, I saw such a man yesterday as I was leaving St. Denys. Father de Tormo, did you see the man? He came into the church after I left."

Father de Tormo nodded without hesitation. "I did, indeed, see him," he said. "In fact, I thought he was you because as I came back into the church, he was standing by the candles, where it was shadowed. I did not get a good look at him at first. He asked where Gaston de Russe lived and I directed him to Deverill Castle."

As Dane looked at the priest curiously, Cort spoke. "A man in white was here last night," he said. "I did not think much of it until you mentioned him, but I was checking the posts this morning and the sentries from the night watch told me of the man in white who had left just as they were sealing the gates. They called to him and told him to come back, but he disappeared into the night."

Dane was starting to piece things together. "So the man who went to St. Denys last night came to Deverill and told my father that I had sent him," he said, looking between the priest and Trenton. "Why? Why would he do that?"

The more Dane and the others pondered the situation, the more Father de Tormo had an outlandish idea occur to him. He was a priest; his life was built on faith. He'd seen so much strife in this world, but he'd also seen the good of it. He'd seen many, many people light prayer candles, but had he actually seen prayers answered? He thought so. What had he told Dane last night?

Your love for the man will cause God to hear you loudly.

Perhaps, that had been true. Perhaps, he'd been more correct than he realized. In looking at Gaston this morning, de Tormo was willing to go on that faith.

"Dane," he muttered, his gaze on Gaston. "Did your father's mysterious physic have a name?"

Dane nodded. "He said his name was Raphael."

De Tormo's breath caught in his throat. "The archangel of physics and healing."

Dane looked at him curiously. "What did you say?"

De Tormo looked at him. "I said that Raphael is the archangel of physics and healing," he said. "Mayhap, God listened to your prayers, after all. It would be easy to doubt such a thing. But considering that your father is on his feet and looking better than he has in years, you may want to consider that God, in fact, heard your prayers and He answered them."

Dane looked at the man in shock. It would have been simple to discount him, a fantasy of a zealot. But somehow, given what he was seeing before him in his father's healthy stance, Dane couldn't think of any other explanation, either. Oddly enough, what de Tormo said made a hell of a lot of sense.

"My father told me that Raphael said I had sent him," he said. Then, his eyes widened. "I summoned him with my prayers?"

De Tormo smiled; he couldn't help it. "It is as good an explanation as any," he said. "They say that Christmas Eve is when angels walk the earth. Mayhap, we have been witness to such an event. In any case, we should not question it. We should rejoice and give thanks that your father has lived to see another day."

Dane, Trenton, and Cort couldn't have agreed more. As de Tormo headed over to greet Gaston, the three of them watched as the priest was pelted by some well-aimed snowballs. It was a great mystery to them all, perhaps the greatest mystery they had ever faced. But as de Tormo said, it was not up to them to question why. Perhaps a miracle had, indeed, occurred and they would, indeed, give thanks and rejoice that their father lived to see another day.

In the years to come, the children of Gaston de Russe, Dane and Trenton included, would speak of that Christmas Day when their father was given the greatest gift of all – a true and righteous miracle that all of the physics in London couldn't explain away. Gaston's cancerous throat had somehow gone into remission, and no one seemed to know how or why.

But Dane and Trenton knew.

It was a matter of a little faith… and, perhaps, a wish upon that bright and shining Christmas star on a night when angels walked the earth.

CঃঃTHE END ৩০

ABOUT KATHRYN LE VEQUE

Medieval Just Got Real.

KATHRYN LE VEQUE is a USA TODAY Bestselling author, an Amazon All-Star author, and a #1 bestselling, award-winning, multi-published author in Medieval Historical Romance and Historical Fiction. She has been featured in the NEW YORK TIMES and on USA TODAY's HEA blog. In March 2015, Kathryn was the featured cover story for the March issue of InD'Tale Magazine, the premier Indie author magazine. She was also a quadruple nominee (a record!) for the prestigious RONE awards for 2015.

Kathryn's Medieval Romance novels have been called 'detailed', 'highly romantic', and 'character-rich'. She crafts great adventures of love, battles, passion, and romance in the High Middle Ages. More than that, she writes for both women AND men – an unusual crossover for a romance author – and Kathryn has many male readers who enjoy her stories because of the male perspective, the action, and the adventure.

On October 29, 2015, Amazon launched Kathryn's Kindle Worlds Fan Fiction site WORLD OF DE WOLFE PACK. Please visit Kindle Worlds for Kathryn Le Veque's World of de Wolfe Pack and find many action-packed adventures written by some of the top authors in their genre using Kathryn's characters from the de Wolfe Pack series. As Kindle World's FIRST Historical Romance fan fiction world, Kathryn Le Veque's World of de Wolfe Pack will contain all of the great story-telling you have come to expect.

Kathryn loves to hear from her readers. Please find Kathryn on Facebook at Kathryn Le Veque, Author, or join her on Twitter @kathrynleveque, and don't forget to visit her website and sign up for her blog at www.kathrynleveque. com.

Please follow Kathryn on Bookbub for the latest releases and sales: bookbub.com/authors/kathryn-le-veque.

Made in the USA
Columbia, SC
17 February 2019